FLY GUY & FLY GIRL

FRIENDLY FRENZY

Tedd Arnold

Cartwheel Books

An Imprint of Scholastic Inc.

Specially for Adrienne

ISBN 978-1-338-82699-9

12 11 10 9 8 7 6 5 4 3 2 1   22 23 24 25 26 27

Printed in the U.S.A.   40

This edition first printing, January 2022

Book design by Brian LaRossa

A boy had a pet fly
named Fly Guy.
Fly Guy could say the
boy's name —

A girl had a pet fly
named Fly Girl.
Fly Girl could say the
girl's name — LIZZZ!

CHAPTER 1

One day, Buzz and Fly Guy
saw Liz and Fly Girl
playing in the park.

"Hi, Liz!" said Buzz.

"Oh! Hi, Buzz!" said Liz.

"Let's climb this tree."

"Sure!" said Buzz.

Fly Guy said —

Fly Girl said —

Fly Guy and Fly Girl
followed Buzz and Liz.

"It's nice up here," said Buzz.

"It's my favorite tree," said Liz.

Fly Guy and Fly Girl said —

WUZZLE
WUZZLE

"Can I join you?" said a boy.
"Sure!" said Liz. "I'm Liz."
"And I'm Buzz," said Buzz.
"I'm Carlos," said the boy.

"I like to bring my pet to the park," said Carlos. "This is my lizard named Annie."

"We have our pets here, too,"
said Buzz. "This is Fly . . .
huh? He's gone!"

"That's funny," said Liz.
"Fly Girl is gone, too!"

CHAPTER 2

High up in the tree, Fly Guy and Fly Girl were hiding. They looked down at Carlos and his pet.

Fly Guy said —

Fly Girl said —

Meanwhile, back at the branch, Buzz said, "Where are they?" Liz said, "Maybe they hid because lizards eat flies."

"No!" said Carlos.
"Annie wouldn't do that.
She's sweet. Just look at her.
She's . . . huh? She's *gone!*"

High up in the tree, Fly Guy and Fly Girl both said —

They couldn't see Annie anywhere.

Meanwhile, back at the branch, Liz and Buzz cried, "What if Annie is trying to find our flies and eat them?"

Carlos said, "No! I feed her well! And I never feed her flies. So, relax!"

High up in the tree, Fly
Guy and Fly Girl heard
something behind them.

19

Meanwhile, back at the branch, Buzz asked, "So, what exactly *do* you feed Annie?"

"Stuff," said Carlos. "You know . . . like . . . maggots."

Buzz and Liz screamed, "Maggots are BABY FLIES!!!" Carlos cried, "How am I supposed to know that?"

High up in the tree, Fly Guy and Fly Girl surprised Annie.

CHAPTER 3

Annie fell out of the tree. At the last second, Fly Guy and Fly Girl let go.

SPLAT

OOF!

Annie jumped right up
and chased them. Fly Guy
spotted one of his favorite
places. Fly Girl followed.

They hid in slimy picnic trash. Fly Guy asked —

Together, they peeked out. Fly Girl cried —

Annie found them! Fly Girl grabbed a greasy french fry and threw it.

27

Fly Guy and Fly Girl
threw every french fry they
could find at Annie.

Meanwhile, back at the branch,
Carlos said, "I'm sorry.
I didn't know I'd meet new
friends who had pet flies."
Buzz said, "It's not your fault.
But what do we do now?"

Just then, Annie climbed onto the branch.

Liz said, "We all made new friends today!"